The Bride's Christmas Family

D1527773

©2024 by Stella Clark

Contents

Chapter 1

"Do you have the potatoes ready to go yet?" Mrs. McNamara asked as she hurried back into the kitchen. "Everyone will be in the dining room soon. I can already hear them moving about in their rooms."

So could Daisy Miller as she finished up the mashed potatoes. Her feet ached and her ankles were swollen. Her eyelids felt as though she hadn't slept for days. The only saving grace was that the sickness that greeted her every day was always long over by the evening, making supper a much easier meal to cook than the rest. "Just about."

"Good. I can't have anyone saying they had a late meal at McNamara's Boarding

House." The older woman pulled a stack of plates out of the china cabinet. "Our reputation depends on it, but of course you know that."

Summoning the very last bit of strength she had left, Daisy whipped up the mashed potatoes and scooped them into a serving bowl. Together with the rolls, green beans, and stew, the boarders would have a fine, cozy meal to greet them. She carried the bowls out to the dining room one by one, unable to carry any more than that, while her employer fussed about the place settings.

"I really think we need to get some new plates." She chewed her lower lip as she looked over the table. "A few of these are starting to get chipped. It's because of that girl I hired last year to help with washing up.

She just banged them around in the sink without a care in the world."

Lewis McNamara wandered in just then, and he gave his wife a scowl. "The plates are fine, Ann. It's not as though the president is coming for dinner."

"That doesn't mean our boarders wouldn't want to be treated like he is," his wife countered. "There's a reason that all our rooms are full, Lewis, and it isn't because of your pleasant demeanor."

With an impatient harumph, Lewis disappeared through the door.

"I'd send him right back to that oil refinery if I thought I could pry him out of this house," Mrs. McNamara said as she helped set out the serving dishes. "He was plenty happy to let me open this place up and provide a place for workers once he decided to retire, but now all he does is shuffle around and complain! Oh, but I shouldn't speak like that in front of you. I'm sorry."

"No, it's all right," Daisy insisted as she straightened some of the silverware, knowing it would make Mrs. McNamara happy. "Ronald has been gone for a few months now, and I've learned very quickly that I can't be too sensitive about who says what about their husbands, living or dead. I have to believe that God brings us home when He's ready. Ah, I hear them coming down the stairs. I'd better get dessert finished."

She hurried back into the kitchen before the first tenant could make it into the dining room. It wasn't required that she keep herself hidden, but neither did she enjoy the curious stares that her growing belly always earned her. It was getting harder to hide her figure with her skirts and an apron, and curiosity always won out over discretion.

The kitchen was quiet compared to the noise that was filling the dining room as everyone took their seats, and Daisy was glad for the refuge. She checked on the pie, happy to see that the upper crust had just turned golden brown, and set it out to cool. Daisy frowned at the growing pile of dishes in the sink. She was the cook, yes, but that meant that practically every other duty in the kitchen fell to her as well. There was no longer a scullery maid after Mrs. McNamara's displeasure with the last one, and the homeowner herself was busy with cleaning and laundry.

Her stomach rumbled, and Daisy knew she could only last so long on her feet without another meal. She took the plate she'd made and set aside for herself and sat heavily at the kitchen table. For a moment, she didn't even bother to pick up her fork. She just enjoyed the fact that she was off of her feet, even though it wouldn't last long.

"All right, all of that's settled." The door swung open and Mrs. McNamara entered.

Daisy jumped up. "I'm sorry. I'll get the dishes. I was just hungry, and—"

"Hush, child!" The older woman took her by the shoulder and pushed her back down into her seat. "I know you will. The pie is done and everyone else is fed, and it's only right that you should eat, too."

Daisy looked doubtfully at her food. This job was difficult on her body, but it was the only thing she had. A small bit of income and a safe roof over her head wasn't much, but she couldn't risk it. "No, that's all right."

"I'll eat with you." The older woman gave her a challenging look before sitting down at the table herself. "Then you can't argue."

"You're very kind to me." Daisy poked her fork into her mashed potatoes.

"My dear, there is a lot of cruelty and unfairness in the world. There are times when we must be strict, or harsh, or demanding. However, there are also times when we must be open and loving. I believe even the Bible says something along those lines, although in a much prettier way than I can say it." She chuckled a bit as she buttered a roll. "You've certainly had your fair share of the former, I believe."

Daisy nodded. Growing up in an orphanage hadn't really given her much of a childhood. "I had to struggle just to survive, even if the matron of the institution was supposed to take good care of all the little ones there. I made my way by being kind and volunteering to look after the younger ones as I got older, but no amount of good behavior could allow them to keep me once I turned eighteen. That's when I married Ronald."

Mrs. McNamara swallowed and shook her head. "It's a shame what happened to him. In this day and age, the factories provide a good, steady income. The work is dangerous, though, which I don't need to tell you. Left all alone and yet with a growing family! I'm glad that you came to me, dear. I hope that it doesn't disturb you too much to be around all of Ronald's former coworkers, but it makes my heart happy to know that we can be a bit of a family to you in your time of need."

"Yes, and I appreciate that." Daisy hesitated. She didn't want to push that notion of family too far, but she knew there was only so much time left. Every day, the clock ticked a little further. "Mrs. McNamara, I'm worried about what will happen when the baby arrives. I'm not sure how to work and be a mother at the same time."

"Mmm." The older woman's lips puckered. "Yes, I've wondered about that, too. You know I'd offer for you simply to stay here. I put on a good show, but this place is barely getting by with the lodgers that we have. I need your room to either be for an employee or a paying boarder."

"I know. I understand." She'd seen how every bit of space was maximized in order to gain as much rent as possible. Many of the bedrooms were split up amongst several lodgers, and even the parlor and the library had been utilized.

Mrs. McNamara tapped her finger on her cheek. "I'll try to help you think of something. Oh, there's the bell. I told them to ring it when they were ready for dessert. I've got this handled, Daisy, you finish your meal. Coming!" In a rush, Mrs. McNamara went back to the dining room.

Daisy was left alone with her thoughts, and they weren't very good company. Ronald had been her saving grace when she'd left the orphanage, but only three years later she found herself in a similar situation. Nobody would hire her with a baby on her hip, and finding a position when one was still in her belly had been difficult enough. An orphanage was out of the question. Daisy wouldn't leave her child to suffer the way that she did.

But they'd both be suffering if they were living on the streets.

When her plate was empty and she heard the residents tramping back to their rooms, it was time to get back to work. Daisy peeked into the dining room to make sure it was empty before she hurried in to gather up the dishes. She carried a load into the kitchen before returning for another, shaking her head over what a mess they'd made. Someone had spilled gravy on the tablecloth, and there were breadcrumbs on the floor. Even a newspaper had been left in a chair. Daisy tucked it into her apron.

She nearly forgot about it as she stood at the sink, long into the evening as she washed every plate, cup, and fork until they shone. Once they were all on the drying rack, she sat down once more, dreading the long climb up two sets of stairs to her little attic bedroom where she would get a few hours of sleep before it was time to get up and do it all over again.

The paper crinkled as she sat down. Daisy pulled it out and set it on the kitchen table, thinking someone might want it back. She stared at it for a moment, too tired to really read the words, until she realized that the paper was open to advertisements for mail order brides. Daisy picked the paper up and read it in earnest now, finding ranchers, miners, and various other men who lived out West and were in need of a wife.

She set the paper down and rested a hand on her belly. Could this be the answer she'd been looking for? Daisy had no qualms about remarrying. Though Ronald had been good to her, they hadn't been in love. Romance would be nice, but right now she just needed to survive.

Chapter 2

"It's getting cold out there, Rosa," Miles Taylor said as he came in the door. He held it wide so that Jonah, his ranch hand, could come in after him. "I hope you've got something for supper that's going to warm the bones."

"You know I do," Rosa said with a smile. "You get those boots and coats off and wash up. Amanda ought to be home soon."

Miles glanced out the window that faced the road. "I sure do worry about her getting back from school. I know it's important for her to learn her numbers and letters and such, but I can't help but wonder if it was the right idea to let her go. I could always teach her here, myself."

Rosa, an older woman in her fifties who wore her steely gray hair in a rock-solid bun on top of her head, shook her spoon at her employer. "There's much more that our dear Amanda is learning at that school besides just letters and numbers. The child needs friends. She needs to know how to interact with folks besides just the ones she lives with. I'd venture to say it's also very good for her to study under someone other than her father. There's plenty you can teach her about ranching, and there's plenty I can teach her about taking care of a house, but she's learning worldly things in that school that we can't teach her here."

"Yes, ma'am," he replied, scratching a hand over his stubble so she wouldn't see the smile he tried to hide. Miles knew he'd done a good job in hiring Rosa Watters to watch over his household after Hettie passed away and left him to raise Amanda on his own. The older woman could cook a full meal out of almost nothing, and she kept their humble ranch home spotless. Most importantly, she always put Amanda first.

"And anyway," Rosa continued as she set a platter of meat on the table, "there's nothing for you to worry about as far as her getting to school and back. Those older children of the Greens seem to truly enjoy picking up so many of the other students in their wagon and taking them back and forth. With all of them traveling together like that, there's not a thing to worry about."

"I'm going to worry whether there's a need or not," Miles admitted. He kept himself from looking out the window once again, but there was no need.

The door burst open and Amanda came in, her cheeks pink from the chilly wind and her braids raggedy from a long day. "Hi, Papa! Hi, Rosa! Hi, Jonah!" She wrapped her arms around Miles.

He hugged her tightly. "Hello, Pumpkin. Did you have a good day at school?"

She shrugged her narrow shoulders. "Yes, pretty much. Miss Egerton got very upset at one of the older boys when he wouldn't stop poking Jenny in the shoulder. Beth says it's because he likes Jenny, but I think it's because he's just very disrespectful."

"Mm. Could be." Miles glanced at Jonah, and the ranch hand was now the one who was trying to hide his smile. The two men had grown up together, and he knew they were both remembering their rowdier days. "Anything else?"

"We talked a lot about Christmas coming up," she said as she unlaced her boots, pulled them off, and set them by the door. "Miss Egerton wants us to do something charitable, maybe for the church or the less fortunate. I'm not sure what the project will be yet, though."

"Christmas already? We've still got a few months," Miles noted.

Amanda took her place at the table and immediately began scooping a mountain of mashed potatoes onto her plate. "She said we have to learn to plan."

"And she's very right about that," Rosa said with a nod. The food was all laid out on the table, and she now took her place. "Planning is important in all aspects of our lives."

"Well, then I suppose I ought to be doing some planning myself. Amanda, have you thought about what you'd like for Christmas this year? Any certain thing you're hoping to find in your stocking on that morning?" Miles began to fill his own plate, wondering if she'd ask for something as small and simple as a hair ribbon or a much bigger gift like a pony to ride to school.

Instead of excitedly gushing to him, Amanda fidgeted in her seat. "Could we talk about it later, Papa?"

He looked over, alarmed. When Miles saw those big pale eyes watching him steadily, a jab of worry moved straight through his heart. "Of course."

Rosa waved her hands. "We've forgotten to say grace! Jonah, would you lead us tonight?"

Later, when they'd eaten their fill and Rosa was cleaning up in the kitchen, Miles sat down in the chair next to the fire. He'd been on edge for the entire meal, wondering what was on his daughter's mind. She sat on the hearth, playing with her doll, and he was trying to decide exactly how he should bring up the subject.

"Beth said that her mother bought some pretty blue fabric at the general store and made herself a dress with it. Beth liked it so much that her mother made her one to match." She twisted the doll's hair into a bun like Rosa's.

Ah, so that was it. "So you'd like a new dress for Christmas?"

She undid the bun and combed the doll's hair out with her fingers. "Her mama also taught her how to embroider. Beth decorated the cuffs of her Sunday dress with little bluebirds that she made all herself."

"I see." A dress with embroidery. Miles could surely find someone in town who could make that happen for him.

"And when the Fosters' house burned and they didn't have anything left to their name, Beth and her mama gathered up all the things they could spare and brought them over." Amanda ran her fingers down the braid she'd just created in the doll's hair. "They do a lot of things like that together."

"Oh." Miles leaned forward in his chair. "This isn't about a dress, is it?"

"Papa." She put the doll down and came to sit in his lap. "I don't remember my mama."

"I know." He kissed the top of her head. Amanda's elbow was digging into his ribs, but he only hugged her tighter against him. "You were only two years old when she passed away, and I don't think anyone would remember something from when they were that young."

Amanda stared disconsolately at the floorboards. "I know. I just wish I did. More than that, I wish I had a mama again."

If a heartbreak could be heard, then Miles' own heart would've brought the whole household running with the crack that now ran through it. Things had been tough as he established his ranch, and they had been even harder once Hettie was gone, but seeing his daughter feeling so sad had to be the biggest challenge yet. This wasn't the pain of a scraped knee or the fear of an unknown adventure. This was a heartache that she'd been carrying around for a while.

"That's all I really want for Christmas," she continued, her voice small and quiet.

"They say that God answers our prayers if they're earnest, and I've been praying really hard. I don't know if He's heard me, though."

Miles pressed his lips together, knowing this was a very delicate situation. "I'm sure that he's heard you, because God listens to children most of all. What we have to remember, though, is that He does things in His own time."

"So do you think he might bring me a new mother someday?" she asked hopefully.

He rubbed his hand over her back. Miles had decided quite some time ago that he wasn't going to remarry. He wouldn't risk his heart again, nor would he risk Amanda's. He had Rosa and Jonah to help him run the ranch, and they were all getting along just fine. But if this was what Amanda wanted more than anything, then how could he deny her? "He might. We'll have to wait and see, I suppose. You probably better get ready for bed. You've got to get to school again tomorrow."

"All right. Good night, Papa."

"Good night, Pumpkin." Miles sat in silence as he watched Amanda run off to her room, but he turned when he heard footsteps behind him.

Rosa had her hands clasped in front of her as she slowly stepped into the room, her head also turned the way Amanda had gone. When the girl was out of earshot, the housekeeper looked at him. "God does do things in His own time, but there's nothing saying we shouldn't help ourselves as much as possible in the meantime."

Miles ran a hand through his hair and sighed. "I don't know what I can do about it, though. You know as well as I do that we have a shortage of eligible women around here. That's why George Graham had to bring in a wife all the way from North Carolina when he wanted to start a family."

Rosa lifted a brow, watching him and saying nothing.

"Right." He sighed and sat back in his chair. "I'll run into town tomorrow."

Chapter 3

"Papa?" Amanda peeked in the door cautiously. "Rosa said you wanted to see me once I was done with my morning chores."

"Come in, Pumpkin." He sat at the desk in his study. The room had felt like an indulgence when he'd built the house but when he'd hesitated, Hettie had insisted. She reminded him that he'd need a quiet place to do the books for the ranch, that not all of his work would be out in the field. She'd been right, of course, but he wished that she could be here right now to tell him whether or not he was right in his most recent decision. Granted, if she were here, then he wouldn't have to do this at all. He held out his arms. "Come sit with me."

"Okay!" She bounced around the oak table that served as a desk and took a seat in his lap. Her head swiveled as she took in all the open letters laid out on the table. "What's all this?"

"Well, you said Miss Egerton has done a good job of teaching you reading and writing. Read this one for me, would you?" He picked up the letter on the left and handed it to her.

Amanda gave him a quizzical look, no doubt because she knew he was more than literate himself, but she turned to the assignment she'd been given. "Dear Mr. Taylor," she began with confidence. "My name is Jane Chapman. I come from a prominent family in Boston, and though my parents are eager to set up a match for me, I would much rather make the choice myself.

I'd like to get to know you, even though we can only do so through letters for the moment."

She broke off and squirmed around in his lap so that she could look at him. "Papa, what is this?"

He rubbed his cheek. Miles had imagined it would be easier to let the whole thing explain itself, but he realized now that he'd been looking at it all through an adult's perspective. There were things he knew that Amanda simply couldn't understand. "Do you remember when you told me that you'd prayed for a mother?"

"Yes," she replied cautiously.

"I wanted to do whatever I could to help God along." His throat was dry. This was so hard. Amanda obviously needed a woman in her life, a woman who could be even closer to her than Rosa was. Miles wanted to make that happen, but what if he'd been wrong in the way he'd gone about it? Would Amanda be disappointed to find that this was the only way?

All he could do was explain himself and hope for the best. "I put an advertisement in a newspaper back East, seeking a wife."

Her brows scrunched together. "You can do that?"

"Yes, and people do it all the time these days. Sometimes when a man comes to the frontier to settle, he can bring his wife with him. That's what your mother and I did. But other times, a man wants to marry and there simply aren't any single women in his area that he is interested in. That's when he would do something like I did and place an advertisement. Women do it, too, when they find themselves in need of a husband."

"Oh." She tapped her finger on her lips. "I thought everyone just met their husbands and wives at church or something."

He chuckled. "Many times they do, or they know each other through their families, or maybe they grew up together. This is just another way of finding someone."

Her eyes widened with hope. "So you're going to get married again?"

Miles tipped his head to the side. "A lot of that is up to you, actually. Whoever I marry wouldn't just be my wife. She would also be your mother. I think it's only fair that you should get to help decide. All of these letters are from women who have written back to me, and they each tell a little bit about themselves."

"Like this one from Boston." Amanda waved the one in her hand.

"Right. I'd like you to read them and tell me what you think."

"Oh, my!" Amanda touched first one letter and then another, her excitement building as she tried to decide which one to read next. "Can I do it right now?"

"I think that would be a good idea." He'd already hung onto the first few letters for several days, and there was nothing Miles would like more than for the whole thing to be over with. He waited patiently with her while she pored over each one carefully, discussing everything from the actual content of the letter to the handwriting to the paper being used.

"Do you want some time to think about it?" Miles asked when she'd made it through them all, only needing to ask for help here and there with deciphering a word or what it meant.

"No." Amanda plucked a letter written in careful hand off the table and held it up. "This one."

"Daisy Miller of Philadelphia. Why this one?" he asked casually, knowing that he'd read this particular letter several times himself. He knew that this would only ever be a practical match. He wasn't looking for love and he didn't want it, but there was something about this woman that had stood out to him, as well.

"She's going to have a baby!" Amanda gushed, clasping her hands under her chin. "I would get a mother *and* a younger sibling!"

"You wouldn't mind having a baby around?" It didn't seem all that long ago that Amanda herself had been a baby.

"No, I'd love it! And I'd get to help take care of the baby. Jenny has a little brother at home, and he's so cute!"

He couldn't help but be touched by his daughter's enthusiasm. "Is there anything else about Daisy that appeals to you?"

"Well, she says she knows how to cook. Rosa does that, but maybe she makes different dishes. And she says she knows how to sew, but Rosa is too busy to show me how."

Amanda was clearly wanting several things that Miles had overlooked, which hurt him all over again. "All right, then. I'll write to her and see if she'd like to come to Montana."

"Will you do it right now?" she asked. Amanda had the dark blonde hair and light blue eyes of her father, but Miles could always see a bit of Hettie in the way her nose tipped up at the end and the way her freckles were scattered across her cheeks.

"Yes," he promised. "Right now."

"Thank you, Papa!" Full of glee, Amanda ran from the room, calling Rosa's name.

It wouldn't be long before Rosa, Jonah, and then the rest of the town knew just what Miles was doing. That was all right, because they'd find out soon enough when a strange woman showed up at the train depot. Miles grabbed a pen and a fresh piece of paper and composed his reply, inviting her to join him as his wife.

He sealed the envelope and sent it off with Jonah, who had already planned a trip into town.

The ranch hand smiled at him knowingly. "Guess we'll have yet another woman to boss us around, eh?" he asked.

"Something like that." Miles returned to his study. There was plenty of work that he needed to do, but instead he sat behind the table and looked out the window. Miles questioned whether he'd made the right decision. He didn't know who this Daisy Miller was. He only knew what she'd claimed in her letter. What if she arrived and married him, but they didn't get along? Miles would only be bringing more heartache for Amanda, and she didn't deserve that. And what was he thinking in trying so hard to create a miracle for her? Yes, Amanda wanted a mother. He could understand, but the girl was young and simply didn't grasp how difficult of a thing she asked for.

He started to wipe off his pen nib but paused for a moment, considering. He could write a second letter to Daisy right now, retracting his offer and saying that he'd made a mistake. Jonah was gone, but Miles could ride the letter into town himself and it would likely arrive on the same day as the first. But how could he disappoint Amanda that way when he'd already made such promises?

The situation was in Daisy's hands now. She was in a desperate situation, so there was a chance she may already have found herself a husband. Miles had also been very clear about only offering her a practical match for the sake of his daughter. If that didn't appeal to Daisy, she'd surely turn down his proposal.

And if not?

He sighed, the burden of it all weighing heavily on him. Miles prayed silently that Daisy would be a caring woman who could grow to love Amanda. The girl didn't deserve to suffer any more than she already had. Everything else would turn out the way it would.

Chapter 4

Daisy's stomach jumped and lurched, but for a change it had nothing to do with her condition. Neither, she sensed, did it have anything to do with the constant movement of the train. It wasn't even the variety of foods that she'd eaten along the trip, some of which that were served at inns were questionable at best. She was quite sure that it was simply her own nerves toying with her.

She took a moment to pray as the train neared their destination, a tiny town that she'd never heard of or seen before. Daisy didn't know how to live on the frontier, not really. She felt herself to be a capable woman, but coming all the way out West felt like coming to a whole new world. What if she couldn't handle it?

Daisy consoled herself in knowing that she could learn whatever she needed to as long as someone was willing to teach her. That still left her concerned about how well she would get along with her new household. She hadn't known Ronald for very long when she'd married him, but at least she'd had a chance to meet him. She truly had no idea what was waiting for her.

As the train pulled to a stop, she was about to find out. Daisy forced herself to be strong as she stood up and got her feet underneath her. She'd read the letter from Miles many times now, and she nearly had it memorized. He'd proposed a pragmatic union, one that would provide his daughter with the mother she needed and Daisy with a father for her own child. That was the most she could hope for, and as long as he fulfilled that promise then she couldn't let herself worry. Daisy waited as the passengers ahead of her filed off the train. She'd accepted that she would marry a man she didn't love. After all, she couldn't love someone she didn't know. She and Miles were strangers who'd agreed to help each other, and that was all.

"Here you are, ma'am. Be careful and watch your step, there. It's a steep one." The conductor took her elbow and helped her down off the train.

Daisy's feet hit the platform, and now there was no turning back. The big Montana sky was even more vast than she'd been able to tell from the train window, doming overhead and stretching on forever. Passengers had flooded the platform, and most of them seemed to know where they were going. Daisy hesitated, a lump in her throat. She'd never even left Philadelphia before, but now she was two thousand miles from the only home she'd ever known.

"Miss Miller?" A young girl came rushing up, her honey blonde braids flying out behind her. She looked eagerly up at Daisy with a wide smile. "Miss Daisy Miller from Philadelphia?"

"Oh, my." Daisy had been full of many feelings, but she was touched with tenderness as she took in this endearing girl. "Yes, that's me. Are you Amanda?"

"Amanda!" A man came charging through the crowd after her, answering a question that he likely hadn't heard. "You can't simply run off like that."

"But Papa! It's her! It's the lady from the letter!" Amanda's slim fingers had already slipped into Daisy's hand, gripping them tightly. "I knew it was her because she looked so nice and so pretty."

The girl might as well have been holding her heart. Daisy knew that Amanda had likely recognized her for her swollen belly rather than her expression, but it moved her all the same. She held out her free hand. "Daisy Miller. You must be Miles Taylor."

"I am." He shook her hand politely. "I'm sorry that Amanda ambushed you like that."

"That's quite all right. It was a very nice welcome." She studied the man who was about to become her husband. It was clear where Amanda got her coloring. His hair was the color of wheat, brushed back from a pair of icy blue eyes. He was strongly built, his muscles showing even through his sleeves. Though he was concerned about his daughter's behavior, and there was no doubt that this was a stressful situation all around, she noticed that he had a kind smile. A small spark of hope ignited in her chest despite all of her hopes to keep it at bay.

"I'll collect your bags," Miles said, nodding politely before moving off to speak to the porter.

"Papa says we're going straight to the church," Amanda offered gleefully. "I told him that we should've had flowers for the wedding, but he says there aren't any flowers this time of year because it's so cold."

There was something about this girl that was just darling. "I'm sure we'll find plenty of flowers in the spring."

If it was possible, Amanda smiled even wider. "I'd like that very much!"

"Was this everything?" Miles returned with Daisy's two cases, one in each hand. When she nodded, he gestured toward a waiting wagon. "We'll go ahead and ride to the church. It's not far, but that seems to be the best idea in your condition."

"Thank you." Miles had hardly even looked her in the eye more than once, and he seemed more interested in the business of getting this all done than in getting to know her. His daughter was far more enthusiastic about the whole idea.

Daisy did her best to put her concerns out of her mind as she climbed into the wagon with his help. Miles had made it clear that Amanda was the reason she was here, so of course the girl would be excited.

The church was small and neat. Daisy had imagined that anyplace this far from real civilization would be rough and a little dirty, perhaps even crude, but she felt a familiar sense of peace as she walked into the sanctuary. There were no soaring ceilings or stained-glass windows, but she knew that God was here.

"Welcome, welcome." The preacher gestured them forward. "I've been expecting you. Miles, you're right on time as always.

Are we ready?" He looked at Daisy expectantly.

She realized that Miles and Amanda were looking at her with the same question in their eyes. She nodded. "Yes."

Daisy stood before the preacher—before God—and thought about the marriage she was about to enter. She felt that spark rise up again. She was only twenty-one and had many years ahead of her. Miles was a few years older, but they could expect to spend decades together. Would that be enough for love to start? Could they find something together that was more than a contract?

She pushed those thoughts down once more, trying to bury them deep. Daisy had always dreamed of falling in love, but she couldn't allow herself to wish for such a thing. She couldn't bear the disappointment if it never came to be, and she only needed to focus on what she *did* have. Amanda had taken her hand again, just as much a part of the ceremony as she and Miles were. The one thing she knew for certain was that this little girl needed her.

"I now pronounce you man and wife," the preacher announced. "May God bless your union. Will I be seeing you both on Sunday morning?"

"No need to even ask," Miles promised with a nod. He brought his daughter and his new wife back out to the wagon and once again helped Daisy up into the seat. "It's about an hour's ride to the ranch. Are you comfortable?"

She appreciated that he was so concerned for her health and comfort when they'd known each other for such a short amount of time. It spoke volumes about him whether he knew it or not. "I think I'll be all right, thank you."

"Why do you keep sniffing?" Amanda asked. She had almost the entirety of the rest of the wagon to herself except for the small amount of space that Daisy's luggage took up, but she was pressed right up behind the seat.

"Amanda, you're being rude," Miles warned gently.

Perhaps it wasn't a polite question, but Daisy could understand why she asked it. She hadn't even realized she'd been doing anything noticeable, but she had to laugh at herself a little. "It's just that the air is so fresh here. Where I come from, there are a lot of oil refineries and factories. They fill the air with a thick, greasy smoke that never really seems to go away. I was used to it, I'm sure, but I could tell the difference the moment I stepped off the train."

"Do you miss it? The city?"

"I haven't really had any time to miss it yet," Daisy admitted. And what was there to miss? Ronald was one of very few people who'd cared for her in any way, and he was gone. Mrs. McNamara had worried about her, but she'd already told Daisy that there wouldn't be a place for her there once she delivered her child. She had no prospects in Philadelphia, but she had a true chance of being happy here in Montana.

Chapter 5

"Have you been to a ranch before?" Amanda had been full of questions during the ride, and though they drew near to the house, she hadn't yet run out of them.

"I haven't," Daisy admitted. She was starting to get tired now that she was nearing the end of her travels. The train ride had been long, and even though the springs under the wagon seat kept the worst of the bumps to a minimum, she could feel the same sort of exhaustion that she had after a long day of work for Mrs. McNamara. It wasn't over yet, either, not really.

"You're going to love it!" Amanda enthused. "Papa, can I show her around?"

His eyes were steady on the road, just as they had been this whole time. Miles had contributed here and there to the conversation, but he'd mostly seemed content to let his daughter run the show. "That would work well, actually. The work around here never stops, and I have some things I need to get to."

Though she knew she shouldn't, Daisy felt a bit of disappointment. This was her new husband, and even if they weren't going to have a whirlwind romance, she wanted him to at least be a little bit enthusiastic about her arrival.

Miles turned the horse down a long drive, and Daisy got her first real view of the ranch. She'd seen the curl of smoke rising up over the hill as they were further back on the road, and Amanda had diligently pointed it out to her, but that little bit of smoke was nothing compared to what lay before her now. She'd only ever lived in the orphanage, a small apartment with Ronald, and then the boarding house. They had been big buildings overall, but there were only very small spaces within them that she could call her own. Now she took in the two-story farmhouse, proudly whitewashed on a slight rise in the yard. Several fluffy chickens pecked the yard, but they skittered toward the barn when they heard the rumble of the wagon. The barn itself was huge, with its peaked roof and hay loft. The roof extended in wings on either side as it reached the walls, making a shaded area for the horses to run in on one side and a protected area for larger tools on the other side. A well and a chicken coop completed the scene, with a rectangle of hard earth that must've been a vegetable garden in the warmer months.

"Do you like it? I think she likes it, Papa! Just look at her!" Amanda wiggled excitedly in the back of the wagon, standing up before it even came to a full stop in front of the barn.

Aware of how focused she'd been on her surroundings, Daisy realized her mouth had been hanging open slightly in astonishment. "It's very different from anything I'm used to."

Miles swung easily down from the wagon seat and came around to help Daisy, but he addressed his daughter. "Let's take her inside to meet Rosa, first."

"Okay!" Amanda's braids flew as she ran to the house.

That left Daisy completely alone with her new husband for the first time. A few birds called in the distance, and the breeze sighed softly in a stand of pines near the barn, but otherwise the silence was heavy. Daisy's legs were stiff and store, but she tried not to let that show. "She's very enthusiastic."

A hint of a smile played on his lips. "I'd say she likes you."

But do you? It was an unfair question, and she wouldn't ask it. A child was happy to make her judgements about people without more than a quick meeting, but adults were more leery. They had to be, and experience had taught them that not everyone was worthy of their friendship. Would it always be like this with him? There was only so much she could learn about him from a singular letter. If she'd had the time, she might've asked to write for a while before she'd agreed to come all the way to Montana. But the growing child in her belly had dictated otherwise.

"This is a beautiful place you have here," she said instead. "Did you—oh!" Daisy paused, her hand automatically going to her lower back as a bolt of pain shot through it.

Miles instantly had his hand under her elbow, holding her up. "Are you all right? Should I fetch the doctor?"

Daisy breathed through the pain for a moment before shaking her head. "I'm all right. I'm sorry."

His face studied hers, looking at her directly for the first time since she'd first stepped off the train. "You looked like you were in a lot of pain, though."

She had been, but now a surge of optimism swelled in her chest as she saw that he was genuinely concerned for her wellbeing. That didn't mean he held any great emotions for her, of course, but he was at least a decent enough man to be considerate of her. "I've had this before. A friend of mine told me that it's perfectly normal, even if doesn't feel very good."

He hesitated for another moment before he nodded and guided her up the stairs to the farmhouse. Miles opened the door and brought her inside, where Amanda was leading an older woman by the hand to the door.

"Here she is!" the girl announced. "Rosa, this is Daisy. Daisy, this is Rosa."

Miles had explained the presence of his housekeeper in his letter, so finding another woman here was no surprise for her. Daisy extended her hand. "Daisy Miller—er, Taylor, I suppose. It's very nice to meet you."

The other woman beamed at her happily. "Rosa Watters. I'm so very happy to meet you."

If Miles was neutral about her arrival, then at least Rosa seemed authentically glad for her to be here. "You, as well."

Miles cleared his throat. "Um, I'll be out in the barn. I have some things to get done. Amanda, make sure you help Daisy feel at home." He slipped back out the front door.

Rosa clucked her tongue once the door closed. "Men are funny animals. I'll have to keep our introductions short. I'm leaving soon to spend a few weeks with my family for Christmas."

"Oh, that's too bad," Daisy replied honestly. There was something about Rosa's warm smile that reminded her a bit of the kinder side of Mrs. McNamara. "I mean, it's wonderful that you'll be with your family for the holiday. I was looking forward to getting to know you."

"There will be plenty of time for that when I get back. This will give you time to get all settled in here with your new family without me underfoot. A new bride deserves a chance to organize her household in the manner she wishes, after all! And don't you worry. I'll be back at the beginning of the year to help you get prepared for the arrival of your little one. I assume we still have some time?" Rosa looked at her searchingly.

Daisy nodded. "I believe it'll be around the beginning of March." She'd counted the days endlessly, especially since she'd known that her condition had put her under such pressure to find a new position in life.

"Wonderful! I can't tell you how excited I am, and Amanda has gone on and on about how much she wants to help out as a big sister," Rosa said warmly as she gently touched the little girl's shoulder.

Amanda, meanwhile, had been hopping back and forth from one foot to another as she waited for the grownups to finish talking. "Daisy, can I show you the house now?"

"She may want to rest," the housekeeper reminded her. "She's had a very long journey."

That was true on both counts, but Daisy simply couldn't bear to disappoint the little girl. She had such zeal for this big change in her life, and it would be sad to see her lose it. "I think I can muster a little more energy. Besides, I need to know where everything is."

"Let's start in the kitchen!" Amanda took her hand and led her through the house, from one room to the next, explaining not just what each room was but also revealing some little detail that nobody but her probably would've noticed.

"This is where Papa likes to sit and whittle after supper," she said as she pointed to the cozy chair near the hearth in the living room. "That's why there are always some shavings on the floor. Rosa sweeps them up, but she says they multiply like mice, whatever that means."

"This is my room." Amanda spread her arms wide to encompass the bedroom on the second floor. "Don't be upset, but it's the best room in the house. Both Papa and Rosa have said so, but we have a very nice room for you, too."

"Papa does all his paperwork in here," she explained in his study. "This is where he told me you were coming, and he let me read all the letters."

"Letters?" This particular explanation caught her off-guard. Daisy knew she'd only written one letter.

"Uh huh. From you and the other ladies who wrote back to Papa. I got to pick you!" As if this was more than enough said about the subject, she bounded out of the room.

Daisy followed, feeling uncertain. On the one hand she was happy to know that Miles was so considerate of his daughter that he let her assist in the process, and of course it was flattering to know that she was chosen out of several. On the other hand, she'd been nothing more than a letter. No wonder Miles didn't seem to think much of her when she was just one of several choices, and any of them must've been the same to him.

Amanda next gave her a tour of the barnyard. "Papa told me I'm not supposed to name the chickens. He said we can't get attached to them, since we'll be eating some of them. But this one is special, so I named her Helen." With the ease of a child who'd grown up in this environment, Amanda scooped up a speckled hen as it ran by.

"And why did you pick the name Helen?" Daisy inquired.

"Because she's got all these ruffly feathers, and she reminds me of Helen at church," Amanda replied simply before she let the chicken rush off after her other friends.

"I see." Daisy wondered if the human version of Helen had any idea about this and whether or not she'd be flattered. She hid her smile and made a mental note that she'd have to meet this Helen when they went to church on Sunday.

After showing her the vegetable patch, the well, the pile of firewood, the narrow path that led to the creek, and the best place to catch grubs to fish with, Amanda finally brought her back into the house and showed her to her room. "This is all yours!" she announced. "I picked out the quilt to put in here for you. I don't know if you like blue, but I thought it was pretty."

"Thank you very much. It's lovely." Daisy touched the thick quilt, assembled from multiple shades of blue. A pretty calico with a floral pattern had been carefully arranged as a border.

"My mama made it." Amanda touched it, too, but she looked at it with uncertainty. "I guess she made a lot of quilts, and she was really good at it. I don't remember her, though."

This girl was going to absolutely break Daisy's heart. "I'm sorry. I don't remember my mama, either."

Amanda's eyes were huge as she whirled to look at her new stepmother. "You don't?"

"No." She hadn't thought about it in a long time, not in precisely this manner. Daisy's life had been so full of other heartbreaks, and once she'd left the orphanage she no longer had time to lie alone in her bed at night and wonder what had happened to her parents. "I was left at an orphanage when I was just a baby. I never knew either of my parents."

"Not your Papa, either?" Amanda hoisted her narrow body onto the bed and wriggled until her leg pressed against Daisy's.

"No, not any of my family. I've had a few people who've helped me out here and there in life, but I've never really had a family in the way that most folks think about it." Now, with a child on the way, she was guaranteed to have at least a little bit of that family. Could Amanda, Miles, and even Rosa be a part of it as well? She hoped so.

"Oh, my." Amanda, solemn for a change, put her hand in Daisy's. "That's sad. I've always wondered about my mama, but at least

I have Papa. He's a good daddy, and I know he loves me."

"I can see that." Daisy had witnessed it even just on this first day of knowing them. There was plenty that she had yet to learn about Miles, but she had no doubt as to how he felt about his daughter. He had a whole ranch here to run, but he kept her as his priority.

Amanda took her hand back, but it was only so that she could wrap her arms around Daisy and press her head against her. "I'm really glad you're here with us."

Daisy took a deep breath and felt her body relax a little bit. She'd had plenty of uncertainty in her life, and there was some still yet to figure out, but she knew right at that moment that she was where she was supposed to be. "Me too."

Chapter 6

"Amanda, I think I need a bit of help from you if you don't mind." Daisy had been thinking about it as she finished her breakfast, eating slowly and thoughtfully. She'd gotten up early and made a meal, glad to find that Rosa had left the kitchen well stocked for her. Miles and Jonah had joined them, but they'd left quickly to get to their work.

"With what?" Amanda licked a bit of gravy from her finger.

Daisy held off on correcting her. There would be plenty of time to talk about manners once they had a chance to get to know each other better, but she didn't want to swoop in and change the child the moment she arrived.

"You've done a wonderful job of showing me around the place, but I wondered if you might also let me know what the usual routine is around here."

Amanda tipped her head to the side and scrunched her brow. "You're a grown-up. Doesn't that mean you can do what you want?"

"Not really," Daisy admitted, "not when I have other people to consider. There's a lot I have to take care of around here, and I want to help the ranch operate as well as possible. I could muddle through and figure it out, but I'd like to know how things usually go."

"Does that mean you'll change it? I heard Rosa say something about setting up your household yourself." Amanda found a stray biscuit crumb on the rim of her plate and scooped it into her mouth.

"I might, but I don't know yet." She'd appreciated that the housekeeper had wanted to give her ample space so that she'd truly feel like the woman of the house, but it was also intimidating. Daisy had run the household while she'd been married to Ronald, but managing an apartment was nothing like running a farmhouse that was part of a ranch. She worried that she'd miss some essential task, something that Miles relied on her to do.

"Well, we had breakfast." Amanda marked the task off on her finger. "Then Rosa washes up all the breakfast dishes. I usually help unless I have school."

Daisy had figured as much, but she could see that Amanda felt important for getting to tell her. "And then what comes after that?"

"Mmm…firewood. Rosa likes to keep plenty in the house in case we get a big storm. There was one year that it snowed a whole lot in just one day, and she had to dig all the firewood out from underneath it. Ever since then, she says, she brings in more than she needs." Amanda picked up her plate and followed Daisy into the kitchen.

"That makes sense." Daisy had seen the long cords of firewood stacked up in the lean-to outside, and she'd been relieved that they wouldn't have a hard time getting fuel for cooking and staying warm. "Then what?"

Amanda was ready with the next answer, having had a moment to think. "Feeding the chickens. They eat a bit of grain, plus whatever food scraps come from the kitchen. Rosa uses that big bowl for the potato peels and such. And we gather the eggs while we're out there, too."

The Taylors didn't live an extravagant lifestyle out here on the frontier, but the abundant resources they had right there on the property gave Daisy a sense of security that she'd never known before. If they were hungry, they had only to walk out the door to find something to eat. "It sounds like we'll stay very busy."

"Yes." Amanda frowned as she put a plate on the drying rack. "There's always work to be done. Papa says the work is never really done. It's always just done for now."

"That's how life is," Daisy agreed. "Still, you can get a nice sense of accomplishment from taking care of the things around you."

"I guess, but…" Amanda trailed off as she dried her hands.

"What is it?" Daisy had always wanted to be a mother. She'd had a bit of experience when she'd taken care of the younger children at the orphanage. They'd looked up to her, and it had irritated the matron that they minded her better. Though she'd never imagined she'd be taking care of a child that wasn't hers by blood, she knew that she could with a bit of patience and understanding. Daisy stopped what she was doing and turned to look at Amanda, giving her full attention.

"Well." Amanda rolled her eyes, looking everywhere but at Daisy. "I know there's always work to do, but I was wondering if we could take some time to get the house ready for Christmas."

Daisy smiled. "That sounds wonderful."

"Really?" Amanda squealed. "When?"

Daisy considered this. She truly did need to figure out how she was going to run this household, but she didn't want to deny Amanda the chance to make the house ready for Christmas. "How about we get the firewood and the chickens taken care of first, and then we'll do something. How would you like to start?"

"A tree!" Amanda announced. "A big one!" She threw her arms out wide to demonstrate. "And really tall!" She jumped as high as she could with her hand toward the ceiling.

Daisy laughed. "We'll do the best we can, but I don't think I'm strong enough to bring a tree that big into the house."

"Papa can," she replied with confidence. "He'll have already gone out to check the fences and should be back up by the barn by then, so I'll ask him to go with us!"

Though Daisy felt a bit doubtful about whether or not Miles would be willing to contribute to such a cozy family scene, she decided that in this case Amanda probably knew better. And if Miles would say yes to anyone, it would be her.

Later that morning, they bundled up and headed outside. A thin coating of powdery snow covered everything, which seemed to make Amanda even more excited than she already was. "Papa!" she called as she raced into the barn. "I need my sled! And you need to get your axe! We're going to get a tree!"

"A tree?" Miles had just brought his horse back inside after a morning of work.

"Yes! A Christmas tree! Let's go!" She grabbed her sled from the corner and ran with it toward the door.

Miles watched her go and as he turned, his eyes landed on Amanda in the doorway. He and his daughter had the same shade of sky-blue eyes, but they were different on him. So much more reserved and cautious. "Are you sure you feel up to this?" he asked.

"I think I'll be all right." In fact, she felt much better than she had when she'd arrived after sleeping soundly on a good bed with a comfortable quilt.

They headed into the wilderness behind the barnyard. Amanda led the way with her sled behind her, turning to examine every tree they passed. "What about that one?"

Miles leaned his head back to look all the way up at the top of the massive tree. "Darling, that's a mature Ponderosa pine. I think it's a bit big to go in the house."

Undeterred, Amanda pressed onward. "How about that one? I like junipers!"

The tree was still very large, and Daisy was fairly certain it wouldn't work. As she looked up the trunk, though, she noticed something besides its height. "There's a family of owls living there. Look, right there in that hole. We couldn't turn them out when it's almost Christmas."

"There's got to be a good one around here somewhere," Amanda insisted, charging ahead.

Daisy scanned their surroundings. There had been a few Christmas trees when she was living at the orphanage, when some kind donor had wanted to make the holidays special for the unfortunate children. She'd never had one in her own home, though, and she was starting to feel Amanda's excitement.

Her eyes landed on a little fir tree off to the right. It was young still, with its branches growing all the way up and down its trunk. It was full and fluffy, a perfect little tree to hold many ornaments. She lifted her hand to point. "How about that one?"

At precisely the same moment, Miles gestured at the very same tree. "That's the one!"

Amanda, seeing that her father and her new mother were in such unison, clapped with joy. "Cut it down, Papa!"

Soon enough, the tree was on the sled. It was no longer light enough for Amanda to pull alone, and she enlisted the help of her father. Daisy walked along just behind them, taking in the crisp air, the fresh whiteness of the snow, and the beauty of a little girl who loved her father. Amanda was full of love, it seemed. She cared deeply not only for Miles, but she also loved Rosa and Jonah as though they were family. Even Daisy, who felt as though she belonged here the least of all, was equally important in the girl's eyes.

"Daisy, get the door!" Amanda said when they reached the house. "Papa and I will carry it in."

"All right." Since she wasn't in a position to help wrestle the tree inside, Daisy complied. She held the door while Amanda carried the top of the tree and Miles the trunk. "Looks like you've got your tree."

"No," the girl insisted with a smile. "We're not done yet!"

Chapter 7

"I think that does it." With some spare boards from the barn, Miles had managed to make a good little stand for the tree. He put the final nail in and stood the tree up, waiting for a moment to make sure it was steady. "What do you think?"

"It beautiful!" Amanda darted forward and gave the tree a hug. "It's even better than I thought it would be."

Miles watched his daughter carefully. She'd always been an energetic, enthusiastic girl, but there was a new light in her that he could swear hadn't been there before. "I'm glad you like it. I'll take these tools back out to the barn, now. I've got to make some repairs out there, anyway."

"Wait, Papa!" Amanda was suddenly in front of him, blocking his way. "You can't go yet!"

He threaded the hammer through his belt loop. "And why not?"

She gave him an impatient look. "We still have to decorate the tree!"

Miles swallowed. He couldn't turn her down when she asked for help chopping down a tree, especially since it wasn't as though Daisy or Amanda could do it alone. He glanced at the door, wanting desperately to get back out to the barn where he wouldn't have to look at Daisy's pretty face. "I thought

I'd leave that to you ladies. I don't even know what we're going to decorate it with."

"I've got that all figured out!" Without another word, Amanda shot up the stairs to her room.

Once again, that left him alone with his new wife. Daisy stood hesitantly near the fireplace. Her dark hair was carefully braided into a coil at the nape of her neck, keeping it back from her face so that her hazel eyes could easily be seen. She had slim, arched brows that made her look alert and intelligent. Amanda may have been the first to run up to Daisy on the train platform, but Miles had certainly noticed her first. His eyes had locked on her face above the crowd, and he'd been a bit shocked when his daughter had run off to greet her.

He knew he shouldn't be ungrateful to have a pretty wife, particularly considering the circumstances of their union but in actuality, it was making things much harder on him than he'd realized.

"Here!" Amanda came thundering down the stairs, breaking the awkwardness between the two adults. "Miss Egerton showed us how to make these in class, but I made some more after I came home."

Miles looked into the small box she held aloft, studying the little paper ornaments. They were cut in the shape of angels, snowflakes, and snowmen, and some of them had been brightened by the touch of a brush and watercolors. "So that's what you've been doing in your spare time. I knew it wasn't like you to just squirrel away in your room all afternoon."

Amanda beamed at him. "Do you think they'll look nice on the tree?"

"I do," he admitted, and he knew at that moment that he was committed to staying inside and helping. "I think we've got some string we can hang them with."

"Here, Daisy. I want you to put this one up." Amanda handed Daisy an angel. "She reminds me of you."

"She does?" Daisy pressed a hand to her heart. "That's very sweet of you. I think it'll look very nice right here. Which one are you going to hang?"

"This one!" Amanda fetched a snowman. They each took turns until all the ornaments had been used, but Amanda wasn't quite satisfied. "It needs something else."

"Do we have any popcorn?" Daisy asked. "I've got my sewing kit with a needle and plenty of thread, so we could make a pretty garland."

As with everything else, Amanda's eagerness propelled them into the next project. Miles fetched the heavy pot and put it on the fire while Amanda retrieved the popcorn from the cellar and Daisy threaded her needle. He thought he might get a chance to slip back out to the barnyard once they got started, but Amanda put him to work holding up the knotted end of the garland while she and Daisy threaded the popcorn.

"I don't want it to get dusty if I'm going to eat it later," she explained.

Miles patiently sat there with one end of the garland, watching his daughter. He had a good suspicion that she'd be happy to eat the popcorn whether it was dusty or not. She liked her dresses and her braids, but she was also a rough-and-tumble girl who ate vegetables straight out of the garden and spent much of the summer fishing in the creek. There was no real need for him to be in here. Was Amanda trying her best to keep him and Daisy in the same room?

His eyes shifted over to Daisy, who was too focused on Amanda to notice. "Here, why don't you try?" She handed the threaded needle over.

"But I don't know how to sew," Amanda countered.

"You don't need to. Just poke the needle through the popcorn, like this. It doesn't have to be perfect. You only have to watch the sharp end so that you don't poke yourself."

Amanda carefully added several pieces of popcorn. "Have you poked yourself before?"

"I certainly have." Daisy laughed, and it was a beautiful sound. "It's going to happen every now and then, so you just do your best."

Her laughter made something move inside him. Miles knew he should look away, but he couldn't. There was much to admire in Daisy. Yes, she'd come here because she needed a safe place for herself and her child. That had been a good motivation for her to make this move and marry him, but he could see just how much of a bond was forming between his new wife and his little girl. There was genuine affection in Daisy's eyes as she talked and laughed with Amanda.

Miles recalled the conversation he'd had with Rosa before she'd left to see her family. The housekeeper had come out to the barn to say goodbye to him before Jonah drove her into town.

"Now, Miles, you behave yourself while I'm gone," she'd said, shaking her finger at him as though he was an errant child.

He'd laughed. "Is there any reason to think I won't?"

"Oh, yes." The two of them had been alone at that moment, fortunately. "Miles, I know that it's going to be hard for you to have a woman around here again."

"You've been around for years," he'd tossed back.

"That's not what I mean and you know it." Rosa was a kind woman, but she was also one to speak her mind. "Daisy seems like a wonderful lady. She's going to be good for Amanda."

"Yes," he'd agreed. "That's why she's here."

"But I think she could also be good for you if you let her be," Rosa continued. "I can tell already that you're trying to keep your distance from her, but I think you ought to give this a chance."

Miles had decided then to level with her. "I know what you're getting at, but I'm not interested. Daisy knows that this is an arrangement of convenience, something that will help us both out. There's no romance between us."

The older woman had eyed him carefully. "And you don't want there to be?"

"No. I was already in love once, and I've suffered for it greatly. I'm not interested in repeating that," he'd said firmly.

"As you wish, then," she'd replied. "But keep in mind that love is not a finite thing. Just because you spent a lot of love on Hettie doesn't mean you've run out. There's always more, Miles. You have a Merry Christmas."

Miles hadn't really paid much attention to Rosa's words, but he thought about them more seriously now that he sat here with his bride and his daughter. Daisy had been married before, and she had a child on the way. If there was only a fixed amount of love within her, could she possibly be so compassionate towards Amanda? He'd never really considered it a matter of running out of love but a matter of not wanting to feel the heartache that Hettie had left him with. The only way he knew how to keep his heart safe was to keep it distant. A man could easily fall for Daisy with her pretty looks, her pleasant laugh, and her way with children. Even the breakfast that she'd made for him this morning could influence someone to want to spend more time with her.

"It's done!" Amanda declared. "Let's put it on the tree. Papa, you hold that end up at the top, and Daisy and I will wind it around."

He did as he was asked, keeping his end of the garland secured at the top of the tree. Amanda ducked and dodged around to wind the popcorn where she wanted it, and Daisy worked to drape it nicely on the boughs. Her hand brushed his arm, sending a fluttering through his chest. This wasn't going to be easy.

Chapter 8

"These smell amazing!" Amanda pulled the sheet of cookies from the oven and inhaled deeply. "It makes it feel like Christmas already!"

Daisy laughed, but she understood the feeling. The Christmas tree, so carefully decorated with those handmade ornaments, had already made the inside of the house smell like evergreens. Adding the cinnamon-and-sugar fragrance of the cookies enhanced the effect, and she found herself feeling much more in the holiday spirit than she usually did. "We still have a little bit to wait."

"I know, but that makes me happy, too." Amanda carefully balanced the cookie sheet on a couple of trivets that Daisy had laid out on the table. She left them there to cool and came around to the other side of the table to help Daisy form more little balls of dough for the next tray. "I like the getting ready part just almost as much as the day itself."

"That's a wonderful attitude to have." Amanda wasn't her daughter technically, but Daisy was so proud of what a remarkable young lady she was. Plenty of children her age would be impatient, wanting only the pure excitement that came with Christmas morning. Amanda, however, seemed to take delight in almost everything. "It's good to enjoy the moment that you're in."

"Daisy, can I take some of these cookies to Miss Egerton? She's been spending a lot of time worrying about everyone else in the community. All us kids at school made gifts for a family that doesn't have much of anything right now, and she's also been caring for old Mrs. Allen. Her husband died, and now she can hardly take care of herself. Anyway, I thought it would be nice if someone did something for Miss Egerton since she's always doing nice things for other folks."

"I think that sounds wonderful. We can pack some up in a box and tie it with a pretty ribbon. Where does she live?" Daisy slid the next batch into the oven.

"Just down the road. We won't even need to take the wagon. And," Amanda's eyes slid slyly up to Daisy's, "if we have time, there's a pond right near there that's probably frozen solid right now. It would be perfect for ice skating."

Daisy couldn't think of a better way to reward the girl for her generous thoughts about Miss Egerton than to let her indulge in a bit of winter fun. "Then I suppose you'd better bring your skates!"

That afternoon, they set off on their mission. Amanda showed her the way down the road, seemingly unbothered by the cold. "She's right down this way," the girl explained. "The Stewarts built a small house when they moved here, because they needed a place to stay for their first winter. They built a bigger place the next year, but they kept the little one up. That's where Miss Egerton stays."

"You know a lot about what goes on around here," Daisy noted.

Amanda's shoulders rolled under her cloak. "I just listen when people talk. I like to know what's going on. Oh, look. There it is right there!" She pointed to a tiny house with a wreath on the door and then charged forward to knock.

When the door swung open, Daisy found herself looking at a young woman who had to be about the same age as herself. Her bright red hair was neatly braided, and matching freckles smattered her nose. She smiled brightly when she saw Amanda. "Well, hello! What are you doing here?"

"My mama and I made you some cookies!" Amanda announced, holding the box aloft for her teacher.

"How very kind of you!" Miss Egerton enthused as she took the box. She looked up at Daisy. "I'm Tina Egerton. It's nice to meet you."

"Daisy Taylor." She almost misspoke and said her former surname of Miller. It would take some time to adjust to that. It was difficult to keep track of her own tongue when she was so focused on what Amanda had just said.

"Amanda is a wonderful student, you know. She's always paying attention, and she truly does her best on every assignment. I only wish every student would put that much effort into everything they do."

"Thank you. That's good to know." Daisy smiled, and she wondered if Tina had any idea that she wasn't truly Amanda's mother at all.

"Would you two like to come in for some tea?" Tina held the door wide, ushering them in off the threshold. "It's so chilly out there!"

"I don't mind," Amanda replied, though she bounded into the little house.

"Have a seat. I'm afraid I don't have much to offer here, but it's nice to have company." A warm fire was already going, and Tina put the kettle on before she took three mugs down from a hook. "Daisy, Amanda tells me that you just moved here from Philadelphia."

"Miss Egerton showed me where Philadelphia was on the map," Amanda volunteered.

Ah, so Amanda *had* been talking about their home situation at school. Daisy was happy to know that she wasn't something shameful that her stepdaughter tried to hide. "Yes, just a short time ago. And where are you from?"

The two women fell into a pleasant conversation about many things, with Amanda piping in every now and then, and by the time they left, Daisy knew she had a new friend in the community. She was smiling as they walked to the pond, where Amanda hastily tied on her ice skates and raced out onto the frozen water.

The ice was slicker than she'd thought, and Amanda almost immediately went down. Daisy's body froze with worry, but the girl quickly picked herself back up. "Are you all right?"

But Amanda was laughing. "I'm fine! I guess I'm a little out of practice." She waved her hands in circles as she tried to get her balance, still laughing and smiling at herself. Taking first one hesitant glide forward and then another, she shuffled awkwardly around the pond for a couple of circles. After a few minutes, she was gleefully skimming across the surface of the ice.

Using her gloved hand, Daisy cleared a bit of snow off of a tree stump and made herself a place to rest. Her heart was so light, seeing the smile that Amanda had. She'd been patient while Daisy and Tina talked, not demanding that they get going so that she could skate. And now that they were here, she was thrilled just to have the experience.

There was something else she could feel in her heart, and it was more than just joy and happiness. It was love. Amanda had referred to her as her mother. There was no discussion around it. It had simply happened, and that made Daisy even happier. It meant that Amanda truly felt that way about her. If she had love from Amanda and from her coming child, then she knew she would be content in her life no matter what else happened.

But as she watched Amanda skate, her mind wandered back to Miles as it so often did. He was kind and gentle, and he truly loved his daughter. He did anything that was asked of him and often more. Daisy had noticed that the firewood was often magically restocked in the house when neither she nor Amanda had done it. Though he'd often seemed a bit standoffish whenever they were in the same room together, he often asked how she was feeling and if she needed anything. It was nice to have someone who cared.

And, she knew, she wanted those cares to be more. Daisy had been denying her feelings ever since she'd arrived, not wanting to expect more than she could ever possibly hope for. She loved Miles. It was just the beginning of love, to be sure, but it was something that could grow over time into something deep and wonderful. But would he ever feel the same about her, or would he always keep his distance? It was the season of miracles, but Daisy wasn't sure that even a

Christmas miracle could bring about something so magnificent.

Chapter 9

"It's a bitter one today, Miles." Jonah tucked his face down into his scarf as they faced the headwind on their way back to the barn. "You know I've never been a stranger to hard work and bad weather, but I'm a little worried about what the rest of winter might bring us if it's already this bad."

"We'll make it through," Miles assured him mildly. "We always have before."

"That's true. And I suppose it'll be even easier now that you have Daisy by your side." Jonah turned slightly in the saddle, watching him.

"What are you staring at?" Miles asked.

Jonah snorted. "A man who won't admit when he's in love."

"What do you know about love?" he challenged. "I haven't seen you in front of the altar, or even close to it."

"No," his old friend admitted, "but I think most men in your position would be dancing a jig. I just can't figure out why you're not. Daisy is a real peach, and she's made a difference in the household. You're just turning into an old curmudgeon."

"I don't mean to." Miles frowned, not only because he didn't like Jonah telling him that but also because he knew it was the truth. "It's just hard. I know it doesn't seem like it should be, but it is. It feels like I'm betraying Hettie."

"By making sure your daughter has everything she needs, including a mother?" Jonah asked. "I don't think you're seeing that Daisy is also what *you* need. I knew Hettie, and I don't think she'd be upset about that. I think she'd be happy to know you were taken care of."

"Maybe." The conflict in his heart was great, and he wasn't sure how he was going to overcome it. He'd loved Hettie. How could he love someone else?

As they reached the barn and dismounted, Jonah reached out and took the reins of Miles's horse from him. "You go on inside. I'll take care of this."

"But—"

"Just go," the ranch hand urged. "Have a few minutes with your family before I come in to wolf down all of Daisy's good food."

Miles trudged to the house in a sour mood. Rosa and Jonah found it easy enough to tell him what to think or how to behave, but they couldn't understand what things felt like in his heart. Daisy was a good woman, and there were many things to admire about her, but he refused to fall in love with her. He simply couldn't do that.

As he stepped inside, the warm smell of fresh bread enveloped him. The house was more decorated now than it had been a day ago, with boughs of greenery tied with pretty ribbons clinging to the banister and topping the shelves. A bowl of pinecones sat in the middle of the table. Miles paused as he realized what this was. It wasn't just a house, just a roof over his head. It was a home.

Hadn't it always been a home? Hadn't Rosa done many things to make it welcoming and cozy? Miles knew that she had, but he also knew this was different. Daisy had made it her own, and there was a certain sense of happiness at the heart of it.

Moving into the living room, he saw that the tableau of the happy home wasn't restricted to baked goods and holiday decorations. Daisy sat in a chair by the fire. Amanda was pulled up right next to her on a stool, and they both had their heads bent over a wooden hoop.

"You start by making an x with the thread, like this," Daisy explained. "If you look closely, you can see the warp and the weft of the fabric, where it was woven. That will help you line up your stitches so that they look even."

Amanda held the tip of her tongue between her lips as she tried to imitate the stitch Daisy had shown her. "It doesn't look very good."

"I should hope not, since it's your very first one," Daisy replied with a smile. "I started doing this when I was about your age."

"Who taught you, if you didn't have a mama?"

Daisy gazed into the fire, reminiscing. "There was an older girl, Janet, that I shared a room with at the orphanage. She knew a few stitches, and she was convinced that she could help the younger girls get adopted by teaching them their manners or how to sew."

"Did it work? Did you get adopted?" Amanda asked innocently.

"No." Daisy shook her head. "I didn't, but I did fall in love with the needle and thread. I like the way the thread feels when you pull it through the fabric, and I like seeing the results. It's very satisfying both to patch a hole in a shirt and to make a pretty picture."

Miles felt his heart crushing. Daisy had been through such hardships, and yet she was full of joy. She'd brought that joy to Amanda's life. If he was honest with himself, she was bringing joy back into his life as well. He cleared his throat. "I'm sorry to interrupt."

Daisy jumped, startled, and then laughed at herself. "I was so caught up in what I was doing that I didn't even hear you come in! Are we that late? Have I run dinner behind?"

"No, no." He held out a hand to keep her from rising out of her chair. "Jonah and I finished early due to the cold. Don't rush on my account."

"But you must want something hot to drink," she insisted.

"I can get it myself if I'm that desperate. Really." He sat down across from her to prove his point. As he did, he realized that he hadn't purposely sat down in a room with her since she'd arrived other than to eat a meal together. That had been wrong of him. He'd denied Daisy the chance to feel more comfortable in her new home, and he'd denied himself the chance to get to know her better.

"Daisy's teaching me how to embroider!" Amanda beamed as she pulled the needle through the fabric.

"Not just embroidery, but sewing and patching, too," Daisy reminded her. "Embroidery is my favorite part, but the others are quite necessary."

"I have a dress that needs mending. Can we do that?" Amanda asked.

"Certainly."

"I'll get it." The girl was gone in a flash.

Daisy smiled after her. "She's a wonderful girl. I'm truly enjoying the time I get to spend with her."

"She is, too," Miles replied honestly. "And I'm grateful to you for showing her how to sew. There are many things Amanda knows how to do. She throws herself into anything that interests her. She tried to do that with sewing, as well, but she had a harder time. I'm sure she really appreciates having someone to show her."

"I'm happy to." Daisy took a deep breath, pausing for a moment as she slowly let it out. "I wanted to ask you something, if you have a moment."

"Of course." His stomach trembled, wondering what it could be. He worried that he'd made a mistake along the way, something even worse than keeping his distance from her.

Those hazel eyes lifted to his. "It's only a couple of months or so until the baby arrives. I wondered if I could have your input on picking a name."

"Me?" Miles was taken completely aback by this. "Why?"

"Why not? You've provided a safe home for me and for the child. Thanks to you, he or she will have a father to grow up with. Judging by how well you've done with Amanda, I know what a great favor that will be to this little one. It was my baby before we met, but now, well, I'd like to think of it as ours."

His throat tightened. His heart squeezed even more tightly than it had before. "I'd like that very much," he said roughly. "I admit, though, that I don't have much experience in naming babies. Hettie had picked out the name Amanda before we were even married. I thought it was pretty, and so I simply agreed."

Her giggle sent a thrill along his spine. "That's still more experience than I've got!"

Miles looked at her, and he was tempted to pinch himself to make sure he wasn't dreaming. Everyone else had seen such wonderful things in Daisy. He'd seen them, too, but now it felt like he was getting to experience a whole new side of her. This wasn't just a kind woman who took a motherless little girl under her wing and knew how to make some delicious food. This was also a friendly woman, a generous one with a pretty laugh and a lot of love to give. It was no wonder Jonah thought he was an idiot!

"Did you have any names that you'd thought of yet?"

"A few, but I'm just not certain. I know a lot of people like to name their children after their loved ones, but I don't have any family."

"What about your late husband or his family?" Miles suggested. "Is there anyone who meant a lot to you?"

She tipped her head and glanced at the floor. "It wasn't really like that. We took care of each other, but it wasn't a love match. His mother was elderly and very ill when we were wed, and she never approved of me. She wanted her son to marry someone who had a family, who had heritage."

"I see." But he really didn't see at all. Miles had a hard time believing that anyone could marry this woman and not fall in love with her. He'd tried, and he'd given it his best shot, but he was beginning to see that he was failing.

"What about your family?" Daisy asked. "Are there any nice family names that you'd like to pass down? The baby will have your surname, after all."

Miles was grateful that he was sitting down, or else he'd have had to claim a chair quickly. Another child coming into the world, and it would be his. He'd known this would be the case when he'd written to Daisy, but the reality of it hadn't hit him until now. It sent him reeling.

"Are you all right?" she asked.

"Yes, I'm fine," he assured her quickly, knowing that she should be the one for anyone to worry about. "I was actually just remembering what it was like when Hettie and I found out that Amanda was on the way. There's really no feeling like this. We all come into this world as a single person, but having a child makes you feel as though you have expanded."

She laid a hand on her belly. "Yes, I think I know that feeling well!"

They shared a laugh as Amanda came running back into the room. "Here it is! I'd put it all the way at the back of my wardrobe because I couldn't wear it, so it took me a minute to find it. What's so funny?"

"We're just talking about the baby," Miles explained. Warmth flooded his body to have his family here together, whether they were talking about names or sewing or the weather. "We're trying to think of names."

Amanda made a face. "Definitely not Benjamin, if it's a boy."

"Why not?" Miles asked.

"Because Benjamin is the boy who keeps poking Jenny in the shoulder during class. If you name the baby Benjamin, he might grow up to be just like him!" Amanda explained.

"All right," Daisy said with a nod. "Then that's at least one name we don't have to worry about. Now, is this fallen hem the only thing wrong with this dress?"

Distracted from names, Amanda nodded.

"Why didn't you have Rosa fix it?" Miles wanted to know. "You haven't worn that dress for a few weeks, and I'm sure she could've stitched it up for you."

"But I already knew that Daisy was coming, and I wanted *her* to fix it," Amanda explained.

"I can do that," his new wife agreed readily. "You're going to help me, though."

"Me?" The shock in her voice was very similar to the one Miles had heard in his own voice when Daisy had asked for his help with baby names. "But I don't know how yet!"

"No, but you never will if you don't practice. I'll be guiding you the whole way, through every single stitch, so it'll look as beautiful as you are," Daisy promised.

Amanda blushed, which wasn't something Miles had seen her do very often. "Okay."

Miles had been a fool to think he could keep Daisy at arm's length. He'd wanted to honor Hettie's memory, but maybe Rosa and Jonah had been right. His late wife had loved him, and she'd have wanted him to be happy. She would have been thrilled to know that Amanda had someone who could love her as her own. But how could he truly let Daisy into his heart when there was still so much grief inside?

Chapter 10

Dawn came on Christmas morning just as it did every other day, and yet Daisy knew it was special. She rose early and padded to the kitchen, eager to get a hearty breakfast on the table for everyone. Some chores had to be done, even on a holiday, and she could cook a fine meal to fuel them for feeding the livestock and bringing in firewood. She hummed to herself as she sliced ham left from their Christmas Eve dinner, scrambled eggs, and pan-roasted potatoes. It smelled wonderful. Amanda and Miles must've thought so as well, since they showed up in the kitchen a little earlier than usual.

"Oh, heavenly!" Amanda said when she took a big sniff. "I'll bet nobody else in town is having a breakfast as fine as this one!"

Daisy laughed. "I think I'm a decent cook, but I'm sure plenty of other women are, too. I'll bet everyone is making special meals today."

"I'm sure Jonah is happy to be spending the holiday with his family," Miles commented as he loaded up his plate, "but I'll bet he'll be disappointed when he finds out he missed this."

"You two give me too much credit," Daisy protested, blushing a little as she took her seat. It was nice to know her efforts didn't go unnoticed around here. In fact, she realized, the Taylor home was the first place she'd truly felt appreciated. She'd worked hard in any household she'd been a part of, but never before had anyone gone out of their way to tell her how much they valued her efforts.

As Daisy and Miles talked about the chilly weather and when Rosa would be back, Daisy noticed that Amanda was frowning as she picked at her food. "What's wrong? Do you not like potatoes?"

"I do," the little girl said with a sigh. "I was just thinking that it's so nice for us to have this meal together, but Miss Egerton doesn't have anyone."

This caught Daisy's attention. "Doesn't she have any family in the area?"

Amanda shook her head. "She was brought out here from Missouri."

"Oh, that's right." Tina had told her that much when they'd had tea together. "What about the Stewarts? If she's living right there on their property, you think they would invite her in and make her a part of the family."

Miles looked uncomfortable. "She's a tenant of theirs, but I don't think it goes any further than that."

"Well, that settles it then," Daisy said simply.

Amanda sat up straight. "What?"

"After we finish up here with our chores and our gifts, we should bring some food over to Miss Egerton," Daisy suggested.

Miles smiled and nodded. "That's a great idea."

Christmas had barely begun, and already Daisy could feel the holiday spirit moving through her.

When they were finished eating, Daisy pushed her chair back. "Let's get our chores done, then."

"Do we have to?" Amanda wasn't usually prone to whining, but now she crinkled her brow and swung her feet impatiently. "I want to do the presents!"

"We will, Pumpkin," Miles said firmly, "*after* chores. Do you think it's right to let the animals stand out there and go hungry while we open gifts?"

"Oh." Amanda frowned as she thought about this for a minute. "No."

He took her hand and brought her to the front door, where he placed a hat onto her head and bundled a cloak around her arms. "What we can do, though, is make it all go a little faster. If I take care of the horses, and you take care of the chickens, and Daisy washes the dishes, then we'll be opening gifts in no time. Is that all right with you, Daisy?"

"It's perfectly fine by me."

"All right, then." Miles bent down and scooped Amanda up, throwing her over his shoulder. "I'll just take this old sack of feed outside and give it to the horses. Nobody will miss it!"

Amanda squealed with laughter. "Those horses won't eat me!"

"They will if I roll you in oats first!" he teased as he headed outside.

When the chores were done, the family gathered in the living room next to the tree. "That box with the blue ribbon is for you," Daisy told Amanda. Her heartbeat picked up a bit as she hoped that it would go over well.

"A new dress!" Amanda held it up, her eyes sparkling. "It's beautiful! But where did you get it? You couldn't have had time to make it!"

"I did, though," Daisy replied. "You'd be surprised how quick you can get with a needle when you've had years of practice."

"I love it! I just love it! Thank you! Who's this one for?" She grabbed another parcel from under the tree.

"That's for your father, from me." Daisy was even more nervous about this gift. She'd come to know Amanda well, but there was still much to be figured out between herself and Miles.

"You didn't have to do that," he protested as he gently untied the ribbon and set it aside. His brows shot up as he held up the new shirt. "You made this as well?"

"Is it all right?" she asked. Miles looked a bit confused, and she was worried that she'd done something wrong. "I used some of your other shirts for measurements, so the size should be okay."

"It's more than all right. In fact, I think it's one of the nicest gifts I've ever received. Thank you." He turned around and retrieved the next package from under the tree. "This is for you, although I don't think it compares at all to what you've done for me."

"Don't be silly." Daisy gasped when she pulled a pair of new boots from the box. The leather was soft and supple. "They're wonderful!"

"I noticed that yours were getting worn. You spend much of the day on your feet, so I thought you could use them," Miles explained.

"Thank you. I really can."

He scratched the back of his neck. "Actually, why don't you go ahead and try them on? Then you and I can go outside and see if they work well on the snow."

It was a bit of an odd request, but Daisy eagerly complied. She felt like a child getting such a nice gift, so after Amanda had opened the last couple of gifts from Miles, Daisy tried them on.

He held the door open for her and then closed it behind her. He held his hand under her elbow as they went down the steps, and he kept it there as they crossed the yard and walked out to the wooded area where they'd retrieved their Christmas tree. "How do they feel?"

"I didn't realize how bad my other ones had gotten until now," she laughed, feeling silly at what delight this simple gift had brought her. "With the other ones, I was just glad I had something to put on my feet. These feel like a luxury."

"You deserve them, and so much more." He watched her with a strange look in his eyes, one that she'd noticed earlier but hadn't been sure how to interpret. "I'm glad you like them, but there's actually another gift I'd like to give you."

A bit of snow fell from a bough and sprinkled them in white. She smiled as she ducked away from it, but she stayed close to Miles. "Another one? But you've already been so generous."

"No." He shook his head. Then he surprised her by turning toward her and taking her hands, stopping them on the path where they were surrounded by snow and trees. "That's the problem. I really haven't been generous."

She didn't understand. "You've given me a place to live where there's always food on the table. You've even given me a chance to help raise your lovely daughter. I was so desperate and scared back in Philadelphia, worried that I wouldn't be able to care for my baby, but you've taken all those worries away from me. In fact, you've given me a whole new life."

"But I didn't give you what you really deserved." Miles cleared his throat nervously and ran his thumbs over the backs of her hands. "It's not something I can put in a box and tie up with a pretty bow, but I want to give you my heart, Daisy. I know I said that our marriage would be nothing more than a business arrangement, a practical union. I think we've proven that we're very good at that part, making sure that everything around here is taken care of. But I was scared for it to be anything more. Losing my first wife created such heartache, both because of my own grief and because I had to see the pain that it caused Amanda. I thought if I kept you at arm's length, that I might keep my heart safe. But I can't do it, Daisy. Not with you."

"Oh, Miles." Tears sprang to her eyes. They blurred her vision, and she blinked them quickly away so that she might see the gentleness on his face. It created such warmth inside her, and no winter chill could drive it away. "I thought the same thing. I never had anyone who truly cared for me, who loved me the way that family should. I always dreamed of real love, but I knew that I'd have to put that aside once again in favor of being practical, of surviving. But then I see what a good person you are, how you lead your family to God, how you pay such close attention to Amanda and even to me. You're truly a good man, and I can't help but want more with you."

"Then you have it." He raised her hand and pressed his lips to her knuckles. "I love you, Daisy."

"I love you, too, Miles." Her heart leapt with joy as he pulled her close and pressed another kiss to her lips, his mouth gentle and affectionate.

Epilogue

One year later

Miles woke up early. He rolled over and reached across the bed, but the pillow next to him was empty. He sat up and listened. The sound of pots and pans clanging in the kitchen carried down the hall and through the bedroom door. It was early yet, even for Christmas. He smiled and shook his head, knowing that his wife was once again putting in every ounce of effort she could into making this day special.

After splashing his face in the bowl on the vanity, he pulled on his trousers. In reaching for a shirt, he selected his favorite one. It was the one Daisy had given him for Christmas a full year ago now, a gift that she'd made with her own hands just for him. She'd made a few more for him in the intervening time, but this was still the one that meant the most to him. It was proof he could hold in his hands that Daisy cared for him.

As he made his way into the kitchen, he realized that Daisy wasn't alone. He could hear Amanda's constant chatter. Miles grinned and stepped into the doorway, curious as to what he might find.

"Like this?" Amanda asked. She stood in front of the stove with a skillet in one hand and a spoon in the other, and she looked up at Daisy for confirmation.

Daisy, with baby Sarah on her hip, came over to have a look. "You're doing a great job. You see how they're turning that nice shade of golden brown? That's exactly what you want. Crispy, but not overdone. You can take them off the stove now. Put them in that bowl over there so they don't stick to the pan."

"Okay." Amanda hurried to do what she was asked.

Their backs were still turned to him, and Miles took a moment to admire his family. Amanda had grown so much over the past year. She was taller now, and she kept her hair in one long braid instead of two. The childlike look of her face was starting to change, and she was starting to pay more attention to what she wore or how dirty she got when she went outside to play. She had some time yet, but she'd be a young woman before he knew it.

Even Daisy had changed. A year ago, there'd still been some hesitation and fear behind her eyes, a result of living a life of uncertainty. Now, on solid ground, she was positively radiant. She moved through the kitchen with energy and joy as she guided Amanda in cooking the meal and took care of the baby. She had a busy life as a wife and mother, but she seemed truly happy in her position.

Though Miles felt as though he could stand there all day and simply watch them, he couldn't stand idly by for too long. "Let me take that little bundle of joy off your hands for a minute." He reached out.

Sarah squealed with delight when she saw him. She reached out her arms and practically leapt toward him. Her little hands patted his morning stubble.

"Good morning to you, too," he said, kissing her chubby cheek and earning another gummy smile. "It's your first Christmas, little one."

"That's why we have to show her everything," Amanda explained. She'd finished with the potatoes and was now scrambling the eggs that were already cracked into a big bowl. "Mama says it's going to be a long time before she can help make breakfast, though."

"That's true." Miles tugged her braid and gave her a hug. "There's a lot she has yet to learn about Christmas, but you've certainly been helping her."

"You know," Daisy noted as she added some salt and pepper to the eggs, "we're all still figuring out what our Christmas traditions are going to be. This is only the second year of our special breakfast and our pretty tree, and it's the first year of having Sarah with us. I imagine things will change a bit as we decide what we want."

"That's right! Like Miss Egerton coming over!" Amanda practically shouted. "I'm so excited! I loved taking food to her last year, but it's even better that she'll be coming here this year."

"Me too, honey. She should be here soon, so let's get these eggs in the pan." Daisy assisted as the scrambled eggs were poured into the hot skillet.

"What can I do to help?" Miles asked.

Daisy turned around to face him and looked as though she was going to deny him any reason to help at all, but after a look at his face she changed her mind. "It's probably time for Little Miss Sarah to get out of her pajamas and get ready for company. The girls got me up so early this morning that I didn't have time for that yet."

"Not a problem. Come on!" He jogged through the house, making Sarah giggle on her way to the nursery. The little room was adjacent to the one that he and Daisy now shared. Winter frost on the window made the morning sunshine crystallize as it came through the glass, casting a beautiful glow.

He found an outfit for Sarah in the chest of drawers and dressed her, patiently working with the squirming baby as she giggled and jabbered at him. "You're in a good mood this morning. So am I. How can I not be? I have Amanda, I've got Daisy, and I've got you. What more could a man possibly want?"

Miles cleaned her face and ran a soft brush through her hair, cherishing the little curls at the nape of her neck. Sarah looked just like her mother, with dark hair and hazel eyes. It was early yet, but he could swear she also had those arched brows that he'd first noticed when her mother had arrived. "Come on, sweet one. Let's get back into the kitchen."

Daisy and Amanda were putting the last of the meal on serving platters and covering them to keep them warm. Amanda was bouncing with excitement. "Can I take everything to the table now? I want it to be ready when Miss Egerton gets here!"

His wife's eyes flicked up to meet his when he walked back into the kitchen. "I'll help you, and then I was wondering if you could watch Sarah for a few minutes while I talk to your father."

Though Amanda was obviously eager to get the festivities under way, she always jumped at the chance to be in charge of her baby sister. "I can do that! Will she need feeding or changing?"

"Probably not. It won't take long. There's just something I have to take care of before our company arrives." Daisy picked up the platter of ham and brushed Miles's arm as she carried it into the dining room.

The day had started out beautifully, and he knew they were all looking forward to spending it together. But what could she possibly have to tell him that couldn't be said in front of the children or company? Had something gone wrong, and he'd simply not seen it?

With the table laid and the girls occupied, Daisy tugged on his sleeve. "Can I talk to you for a minute? Outside?"

"Of course." He would give her anything she wanted as long as he was able, but he couldn't drive away the knot of worry in his stomach. They put on their coats and stepped onto the porch. Miles glanced up the road, but there was no sign of Tina yet. "I do wish she'd allowed me to come pick her up. I worry about her getting here if the roads are slick."

Daisy smiled. "Tina is a strong and independent woman. She had to be, if she was going to come all the way out here alone."

"And to teach that room of rowdy students," Miles noted as Daisy guided them toward the path.

"Certainly! She's become a very good friend to me, Miles. I appreciate that we can have her here for the holiday, and I know Amanda does, too. It's kind of funny, really. I came from a huge city full of thousands of people, and yet there was almost nobody I could depend on. Then I moved to this tiny town, and all of a sudden I've got so much."

He slipped his hand into hers as they stepped into the trees. "You're happy?"

"How could I not be?" She squeezed her fingers against his. "Rosa has been like a mother to me, teaching me everything that she knows. Tina is like a best friend and a sister, someone I can truly be myself with. Jonah has been a bit like a brother, always ready to lend a hand. Then of course I have you, and I have Amanda, and I have Sarah, and I have our new little one on the way." Daisy raised herself up on her tiptoes and kissed him.

He kissed her back, but then he realized what she'd just said. Miles stepped back and stared at her, his mouth gaping. "What? Little one? Ours?"

"Yes!" she laughed. "The girls will have a new little brother or sister to play with by next summer, I think."

"Oh, Daisy!" He picked her up and spun her in a circle, unable to contain his pure delight. "This is fantastic! Does anyone else know yet?"

"Absolutely not." She pressed her hands against his chest as he set her feet back on the ground again. "You brought me right out here to this spot on this same day last year to give me your heart. It only seemed right that I do the same for you to give you the news. That means we can tell Amanda together."

"Let's go, then," he urged. "She's going to be so happy that she won't even pay attention to her gifts."

"She'll be happy, but I'm sure she'll still want her gifts," Daisy laughed.

They rushed back toward the house, meeting Tina as she came up the drive. Everyone crowded around the breakfast table for a hot meal and then moved to the living room for gifts, games, and to share the news of their growing family. Hugs and congratulations went all around, and Miles knew they'd be repeating the same process once Rosa and Jonah came back after the holidays.

After a while, when the initial exhilaration had died down, Miles sat in his chair with Sarah on his lap. Amanda played on the floor with the dollhouse he'd made for her. Daisy and Tina chatted like old friends who'd known each other their entire lives.

He was a lucky man. He had a secure home and a steady income. His wife and children were happy and healthy, and his family was about to grow again. These were simple things, but he knew now just how important they were. Miles reflected for a moment on how different his life had been just over a year ago. He hadn't thought he lacked anything, and that it was only Amanda who needed the influence of a mother. They had all gotten much more out of this practical arrangement than they'd bargained for. A sense of peace and contentment settled over him, and Miles knew he was truly blessed with a love that would last a lifetime.

Made in the USA
Middletown, DE
20 December 2024

67792614R00088